CARTOON NETWORK™

SCOOBY-DOO!

THE APPLE THIEF

By Gail Herman

Illustrated by Duendes del Sur

WORLDWIDE PUBLISHING
TM

SCHOLASTIC INC.

New York   Toronto   London   Auckland   Sydney
Mexico City   New Delhi   Hong Kong   Buenos Aires

ISBN 0-439-34115-9

30 29 28 27 26   40   15 16/0

Designed by Maria Stasavage
Printed in the U.S.A.
First Scholastic printing, September 2002

Scooby-Doo and Shaggy jumped out
of the Mystery Machine.
"Like, any pizza around here?" said
Shaggy. "I'm starving."
"Rizza! Rizza!" Scooby said.

The rest of the gang climbed out of the van.
Velma laughed. "There's no pizza here."

"This is an apple orchard," Fred added.

"That's right," said Daphne. "We're here to pick apples."

4

"We're here to *pick* apples?" Shaggy moaned. "Not eat them?"

"That comes later," Daphne promised.

"Like, I'm so hungry," Shaggy said. "I'm going to pick more apples than anyone!"

"Don't be so sure." Velma smiled. "I've read books about picking apples. I know exactly how to do it."

Shaggy looked at her. He was much taller than Velma was. He could reach more apples.

"Let's have a contest," he said. "We can split into groups. And the winners get to eat all the apples!"

"I don't know," said Velma. "This is a big place. Maybe we should stay together. So we don't get lost."

Shaggy pictured apple pies and apple jam. Scooby pictured candy apples and sweet applesauce. "Ro way!" said Scooby.

"Then let the contest begin!" said Velma. Everyone took baskets. Shaggy and Scooby went one way. Daphne led Fred and Velma the other way.

Shaggy reached for apples way up high.

Scooby bent for apples way down low.

One by one, they put them in the basket.

10

A little later, Shaggy checked the basket. "Zoinks!" he cried. "It's empty!"

Shaggy eyed Scooby. "Did you eat the apples?"

"Ro ray," said Scooby. "Rou ate the rapples!"

"Like, no way for me, too!" Shaggy said.

They both shrugged. "Let's start over,"
said Shaggy.
They reached and pulled and picked and
tossed. Shaggy peeked in the basket.
Empty again!

"Scooby, stop eating the apples!" Shaggy cried.

Scooby shook his head. "Rou rop eating!"

"*You're* not eating the apples," said Shaggy. "And *I'm* not eating the apples. So who's eating the apples?"

All at once, Scooby shivered. It was getting cold. The sun was going down.

They needed apples to win the contest. But the apples kept disappearing!

"We have to figure this out," said Shaggy. "Before it is too late."

"Who did this?" Shaggy called out.
"Who?" A voice called back.
Shaggy and Scooby jumped.
Someone was teasing them. But they
couldn't see anybody.

"We should call the police!" said Shaggy.

"*Call!*" said a voice.

They peered into the darkness. Still no one.

"Someone is out there," Shaggy said.
"But we can't see him. He must be
invisible!"

All of a sudden, an apple hit Shaggy
on the head.
"Ouch!"
An apple hit Scooby on the head.
"Rouch!"

"It's an apple attack!" Shaggy cried. Apples crashed down, one after the other. "Run for your life, Scoob old buddy," Shaggy said.

They turned to speed away. But they slipped on wet leaves.

Crash! They bumped into something . . . big . . . tall . . . Giant arms trapped them.

"It's the invisible man!" Shaggy shouted.

They tumbled to the ground in a heap.

Boom! Boom! They heard thudding
footsteps. Breaking branches.
But they couldn't see a thing. More
invisible people!
"It's a whole army!" Shaggy wailed.
"We're goners!"

"Jinkies!" said a voice. "We finally found you!"

"The invisible man sounds just like Velma!" said Shaggy.

Velma pulled a wet leaf from Shaggy's eyes. "It *is* Velma," she said.

"What?" Shaggy leaped to his feet. "You're all here! You must have scared away the invisible men."
Shaggy explained about the missing apples. The voices teasing them. The apples hitting them on the head. The giant arms grabbing them.

25

Velma pushed away two branches. "These are your giant arms. You ran into a tree. But you couldn't tell because leaves covered your eyes."

"*Who! Call!*" the voices said again.

"Hmm," said Velma. "That 'whoooo' sounds like a hoot. And the 'call'? That sounds like *caw*."

"An owl and a crow!" Daphne exclaimed.

Next, Velma picked up the basket. "Aha! There's a hole in it! That's why the apples disappeared. They kept falling out!"

"But what about the apple attack?" Shaggy asked as another apple hit his head. "Ouch!" Fred grinned. "The apples are ripe."

"That's right," Velma agreed. "The wind blows them down. Or they fall on their own."

The mystery <u>was</u> <u>so</u>lved. But now it was so dark, the gang could hardly see.

"How will we find our way back?" asked Daphne.

"Look at this, Scoob!" said Shaggy. "All our apples! In a row!"

"It's like a trail," said Velma. "We can follow the apples to find our way back."

"But," said Shaggy, "how do we know who won the contest?" Velma grinned. "You can walk, eat, and count at the same time." "One." *Crunch.* "Two." *Crunch.* "Scooby-dooby-doo!"